Defoe Abbott Marx Hardy Machiavelli Montaigne Chesterton Cooper Emerson Joyce Austen Hugo Eliot Grimm

Melville Haggard Molière

Stoker Christie Carroll Byron Schiller

Wilde Maupassant Engels Smith Kafka

Garnett Fitzgerald Hawthorne Hall

Goethe Einstein Dostoyevsky Willis

Cotton Kipling Doyle

Baum Henry Nietzsche

Leslie Dumas Flaubert Turgenev Balzac

Stockton Vatsyayana Crane

Burroughs Verne Vinci

Curtis Tocqueville Gogol Busch

Homer Widger Tolstoy Whitman

Darwin Thoreau Twain Scott Plato Harte

Potter Freud Zola Lawrence Dickens Hesse Burton

Kant Jowett Stevenson

Andersen Voltaire Cervantes Cooke

London Descartes

Poe Aristotle Wells

Hale James Hastings Irving

Bunner Shakespeare

Richter Chambers

Doré Dante Chekhov Shaw Wodehouse Benedict Alcott

Swift da Pushkin Newton

 tredition®

tredition was established in 2006 by Sandra Latusseck and Soenke Schulz. Based in Hamburg, Germany, tredition offers publishing solutions to authors and publishing houses, combined with world-wide distribution of printed and digital book content. tredition is uniquely positioned to enable authors and publishing houses to create books on their own terms and without conventional manufacturing risks.

For more information please visit: www.tredition.com

TREDITION CLASSICS

This book is part of the TREDITION CLASSICS series. The creators of this series are united by passion for literature and driven by the intention of making all public domain books available in printed format again - worldwide. Most TREDITION CLASSICS titles have been out of print and off the bookstore shelves for decades. At tredition we believe that a great book never goes out of style and that its value is eternal. Several mostly non-profit literature projects provide content to tredition. To support their good work, tredition donates a portion of the proceeds from each sold copy. As a reader of a TREDITION CLASSICS book, you support our mission to save many of the amazing works of world literature from oblivion. See all available books at www.tredition.com.

Project Gutenberg

The content for this book has been graciously provided by Project Gutenberg. Project Gutenberg is a non-profit organization founded by Michael Hart in 1971 at the University of Illinois. The mission of Project Gutenberg is simple: To encourage the creation and distribution of eBooks. Project Gutenberg is the first and largest collection of public domain eBooks.

Tired Church Members

Anna Bartlett Warner

Imprint

This book is part of TREDITION CLASSICS

Author: Anna Bartlett Warner
Cover design: Buchgut, Berlin – Germany

Publisher: tredition GmbH, Hamburg - Germany
ISBN: 978-3-8472-3867-6

www.tredition.com
www.tredition.de

Copyright:
The content of this book is sourced from the public domain.

The intention of the TREDITION CLASSICS series is to make world literature in the public domain available in printed format. Literary enthusiasts and organizations, such as Project Gutenberg, worldwide have scanned and digitally edited the original texts. tredition has subsequently formatted and redesigned the content into a modern reading layout. Therefore, we cannot guarantee the exact reproduction of the original format of a particular historic edition. Please also note that no modifications have been made to the spelling, therefore it may differ from the orthography used today.

TIRED CHURCH MEMBERS.

BY

ANNA WARNER,

"So two or three cities wandered unto one city, to drink water; but they were not satisfied: yet have ye not returned unto me, saith the Lord." — Amos iv. 8.

"Choked with cares and riches and pleasures of this life." — Luke viii. 14.

CONTENTS.

TIRED CHURCH MEMBERS

I suppose one never goes heartily into any bit of Bible study, without finding more than one counted upon. And so for me, searching out this subject of Christian amusements some curious things have come to light. As for instance, how very little the Bible says about them at all. It was hard to find catchwords under which to look. "Amusement"? there is no such word among all the many spoken by God to men. "Recreation"? — nor that either; and "game" is not in all the book, and "rest" is something so wide of the mark (in the Bible sense, I mean) that you must leave it out altogether. And "pastime"? ah, the very thought is an alien.

"This I say, brethren, that the time is short." [1]

Redeem it, buy it up, use it while you may, — such is the Bible stand-point. It flies all too quickly without your help.

"My days are swifter than a weaver's shuttle." [2]

"Pass the time of your sojourning here in fear." [3]

Not in frolic. So you can see that I was puzzled. However, by patiently putting words together, noting carefully the blanks as well, some things become pretty plain; and the vexed question of Christian amusements is answered clearly enough for those who are willing to know. But as we go on searching and comparing, think always of the command once given and never repealed:

"He that hath an ear, let him hear what the Spirit saith unto the churches." [4]

For we call ourselves Christians, — that "people of laws divers from all other people"; and now we are consulting our statute book.

You think, then, — says somebody, — that Christians are to do nothing but work, work, from morning to night: that the Bible forbids all play and all pleasure? No, I think nothing of the sort. But let us see what it really does say. "To the law and to the testimony,"—and abide by them.

To begin then where most of all, perhaps, the old and the modern times are like each other,—feasts have always been in vogue and always permitted; only for Christians, like all else that concerns them, with a special set of regulations as to time, manner, and behaviour. You do not think of this when you dress for your dinner party: you did not suppose the Bible meddled with such things. Nay, it "meddles" (if you call it so) with the very smallest thing a Christian can do.

The feasts of old time were in all essentials so like the feasts of to-day, that not all the changes of race, dress, and viands can much confuse the likeness. There is the great baby celebration for Isaac,[5] and the wedding feast for the daughter of Laban,[6] and the impromptu set-out in Sodom wherewith Lot thought to entertain the angels.[7] There are the great gatherings of young people over which Job was so anxious;[8] and the yearly sacrifice at the house of Jesse "for all the family," [9] reminding one of our Thanksgiving.

Then follow state dinners of amity between two contracting powers; as when Isaac feasted Abimelech,[10] and David feasted Abner.[11] Then court entertainments: the birthday feast of Pharaoh to all his servants, when he lifted up one and hanged another, and the birthday feast of Solomon which marked his entrance upon a new life of duty, opportunity, and promise, and which he kept like a young heir coming of age.

These are all well known to us: and alas, so also are the feasts of social excess, like those of Nabal;[12] and the idolatrous feasts of the men of Shechem,[13] and of the king of Babylon;[14] wherein men praise only "the gods of gold, and of silver, of brass, and of iron, of wood and of stone."

"And the harp, and the viol, the tabret, and pipe, and wine, are in their feasts: but they regard not the work of the Lord, neither consider the operations of his hands." [15]

"A feast is made for laughter,"—but this laughter is "mad"; utterly interdicted to all those who would "live soberly, righteously, and godly" in this world.[16] Such "revellings" are classed among "those works of the flesh which are manifest"; there can be no question about them: the "revellings, banquetings," [17] for which "the time past of our life may suffice us." [18] That time when we were without God in the world, walking as other Gentiles walk. With all such "recreations" the true Israel have absolutely nothing to do.

Does it follow then that a Christian must stand aloof from all festivities that are not wholly among Christian people? Not quite that. "I am a companion of all them that fear thee," said David,[19] and it certainly looks ill for a man if his habit is the other way. Yet there are exceptions, there must be,—else, says the apostle, "ye must needs go out of the world." [20] But like everything else for you and me, it is all within regulations. First as to the going.

"If any of them that believe not bid you to a feast, and ye be disposed to go—" [21]

And then follows the first rule. Whatsoever you can do there Christian-wise; whatsoever you can join in that will not implicate you as a possible worshipper of *his* idol that bade you—even the god of this world—that do. But otherwise there is the strictest hands-off! And for two reasons.

"Eat not for his sake that shewed it, and for conscience sake." [22]

No matter if it be something as simple as eating and drinking. That is the instance given by the apostle, the eating of meat which had been first offered to an idol. And just as once the missionaries in a far off Eastern island never tasted beef for two whole years, because they could get none which they were sure had not been so offered; in like manner are you called upon to absolutely let alone everything which may cast even a doubt upon your loyalty to your Master.

Can you go to the entertainment so, keeping your garments spotless? Can you go as the Lord did?

"And Levi made him a great feast in his own house; and there was a great company of publicans and others that sat down with them." [23]

Pharisees murmured, but the Lord knew why he went.

"And Jesus answered them, They that are whole need not a physician; but they that are sick." [24]

If you can go thus, to do your Master's work; mingling with his enemies to win them for his friends; seeking their company not for their wealth and place, but rather because of their deepest need and danger; not for their gaiety, but for the abounding joy you would fain make known to them out of your own heart-store: then I should say again: "If any of them that believe not bid you to a feast, and ye be disposed to go,"—*go!*

But beware of compromises,—that specious temptation not to make religion disagreeable. It can never be really that if it is the true thing,—a burning fire, a shining light,—but some one has well said: "When religion loses its power to repel, it loses also its power to attract." It must be intense, active, clear enough to do both. "The disciple is not above his Master. If they have called the Master of the house Beelzebub, how much more them of his household"![25]

And it is only as an uncompromising servant of the Lord Jesus, that you can ever hope to do anything for him. On all days, in all places, you must count yourself on duty and under orders. You cannot pledge a man in the wine cup to-night, and to-morrow plead with him to escape for his life. You cannot join in the "foolish talking and jesting, which are not convenient," [26] and afterwards reason of "righteousness, temperance, and judgment to come": or if you do, people will not listen. You will find that, like Lot, you have "lost your spiritual credit." "He seemed as one that mocked, to his sons-in-law."

"I had dined every week all winter with Dr. — —," said a lady to me, "and never guessed that he was a clergyman till yesterday!" Johnson said of Burke, that "you could not stand with him five minutes under a gateway in a shower of rain, without finding out that he was an extraordinary man,"—and how long shall it take people to learn that you are a Christian?—one bought back from slavery, called to be a saint, heir of a kingdom? Ah, how ready men are to parade their worldly honours; their orders of merit and badges of bravery; but leave their Christian colours at home, and hide their uniform with a pair of the world's overalls! Alas!—"If the trumpet give an uncertain sound, who shall prepare himself for battle?" [27]

Yes, if you can go into mixed society as the Lord went, then go. But otherwise, for your own enjoyment, a different model is set.

"Then Jesus, six days before the passover, came to Bethany, where Lazarus was which had been dead, whom he raised from the dead. There they made him a supper; and Martha served; but Lazarus was one of them that sat at the table with him. Then took Mary a pound of ointment of spikenard, very costly, and anointed the feet of Jesus, and wiped his feet with her hair; and the house was filled with the odour of the ointment." [28]

How exquisite the picture! how rare the intercourse, how precious the results! A few of the Lord's own people met together with the Lord himself; the one expensive thing mentioned being bought for him. It was only "a supper"; and there were sorrows before them, and sorrows behind, and only the spikenard was "very costly,"—that consecration to God which gives him all we have: but its fragrance filled the house. And not all Arabia was ever so perfumed.

And must Christians give no other feasts but such as that? some one may ask. There is another sort mentioned, nay even insisted upon; but if the first looks to you dull, the second will seem— impossible! You will find a full description of it in Luke xiv. 13. And so far as I know, this is the only sort of great entertainment that Christians are encouraged to give; ruling out in toto the tit-for-tat customs of modern society. "For they cannot recompense thee." But it also spares you the perplexing question of full returns, for *these* people have given you nothing. Only the Lord has given,—and now bids you keep open house for him in his absence. And do you see? the great Master of assemblies will count the invitations as given to himself, and will one day make a royal return for them all when he cometh in his kingdom. "They cannot recompense thee." [29] What!—never invite your friends unless they happen to be poor? O, yes indeed,—invite them, enjoy them, make much of them, precious things as friends are; yet *spend* the most on the portionless lives that are all around you. There are fancy fountains in the rich man's grounds, throwing up jets of water just to catch the sunlight: let your small rills of refreshment flow silently to places where the tide is out and the streams run dry.

"They cannot recompense thee; but thou shalt be recompensed at the resurrection of the just." [30]

And as soon as you make ready a blessing—not a compliment—in your hand, unfashionable dresses will not matter, untutored tongues will sound sweet; and your feast will be all glorified, for the Lord himself will be there.

"Go your way, eat the fat and drink the sweet, and send portions unto them for whom nothing is prepared." [31]

"The Levite, the stranger, the fatherless, and the widow," [32]—"the poor that are cast out" [33]—these were Israel's special charge under the law. But the gospel gives deeper work.

"When thou makest a dinner or a supper, call not thy friends, nor thy brethren, neither thy kinsmen, nor thy rich neighbours; lest they also bid thee again, and a recompense be made thee. But when thou makest a feast call the poor, the maimed, the lame, the blind; and thou shalt be blessed, for they cannot recompense thee; for thou shalt be recompensed at the resurrection of the just." [34]

The Lord dates the note of payment far ahead, but indeed I think he is better than his word, and deals out much coin as we go along; it is such wonderful pleasure to fill an empty cup! This is "recreation," true and sweet; for of all the refreshments from one's own toil and sorrow, I think ministering to other people is about the best.

I have said nothing—is it needful to say aught?—of the Bible rules for *behaviour* at a feast. One is ready to imagine that *Christians* do only that which is "lovely, and of good report." Yet notice a few things.

"They love the uppermost rooms at feasts," [35] was spoken of the Pharisees; but to his disciples Christ said: "Whosoever will be chief among you, let him be your servant." [36]

"When thou art bidden, go and sit down in the lowest room." [37]

Other things follow close and easily upon that.

"Be courteous."—

"Let your moderation be known unto all men."

"Whether therefore ye eat or drink, or whatsoever ye do, do it all to the glory of God."

And to people with hearts so set, that other vexed question of dress will be easy; for all will be "clothed with humility";[38] and the spotless garments will so far outshine the pearls and costly array, that no one will miss them, nor wish them there.[39]

[1] I Cor. vii. 29.

[2] Job vii. 6.

[3] I Pet. i. 17.

[4] Rev. iii. 22

[5] Gen. xxi. 8.

[6] Gen. xxix 35.

[7] Gen. xix. 3.

[8] Job i. 7.

[9] I Sam. xx. 6.

[10] Gen. xxvi. 30.

[11] II Sam. iii. 20

[12] I Sam. xxv. 26.

[13] Judges ix. 27.

[14] Dan. v. 1.

[15] Isa. v. 12.

[16] Titus ii. 12.

[17] Gal. v. 21.

[18] I Pet. iv. 3.

[19] Ps. cxix. 63.

[20] I Cor. v. 10.

[21] I Cor. x. 27.

[22] I Cor. x. 28.

[23] Luke v. 29.

[24] Luke v. 29.

[25] Matt. x. 25.

[26] Eph. v. 4.

[27] I Cor. ii. 8.

[28] John xii. 1-3.

[29] Luke xiv. 14.

[30] Luke xiv. 14.

[31] Neh. viii. 10.

[32] Deut. xiv. 27.

[33] Isa. lviii. 7.

[34] Luke xiv. 12, 13.

[35] Matt. xxiii. 6.

[36] Matt. xx. 27.

[37] Luke xiv. 10.

[38] I Pet. v. 5.

[39] Sir Matthew Hale thus charged his grandchildren: "I will not have you begin or pledge any health; for it is become one of the greatest artifices of drinking, and occasions of quarrelling in the kingdom. If you pledge one health, you oblige yourself to pledge another, and a third, and so onward; and if you pledge as many as wilt be drunk, you must be debauched and drunk. If they will needs know the reasons of your refusal, it is a fair answer: 'That your grandfather that brought you up, from whom, under God, you have the estate you enjoy or expect, left this in command with you, that you should never begin or pledge a health.'"

"What do you mean by 'the world'?" said a gentleman to me. "I suppose of course you rule out music and painting." So people judge; taking for granted that whatever is pleasant, religion makes wrong. Rule out music?—why it exorcised Saul's evil spirit! Yet even for the enjoyment of sweet sounds there are laws and limitations.

It will be a good day when our so-called sacred music (much of it) more nearly resembles that of old time and has less kinship with the title of a little book yclept "Rhymes and Jingles." A paid choir (no objection to that, if you can buy up their hearts as well) an operatic organist, a silent, criticising congregation. Is there much praise in that? much worship? much refreshment for a tired heart? Look how it was when the ark of God, the visible sign of his presence, was brought home to Jerusalem,—all took part in the music, from the king down; and did it *unto God.*

"And David and all Israel played before God with all their might, and with singing, and with harps, and with psalteries, and with timbrels, and with cymbals, and with trumpets." [1]

"The singers went before, the players on instruments followed after; among them were the damsels playing with timbrels. Bless ye God in the congregations, even the Lord, from the fountain of Israel." [2]

Not much like a quartette and its mute audience! Or how does this compare, with the way we hand over the praise to some who do not even profess to feel it?

"And David spake to the chief of the Levites to appoint their brethren to be singers with instruments of music, psalteries and harps and cymbals, sounding, by lifting up the voice with joy." [3]

There is not much "joy" like that behind most of the choir curtains in our day; but by such means one would be pretty sure of good music. We are not told whether the women took part in the ordinary public music in the temple; but on all special occasions of deliverance and thanksgiving they had their full share. We people in this Western world are so silent in our joy as in our grief,—as apt to bow the head for gladness as for sorrow,—we know nothing like those grand spontaneous bursts of music that once resounded on the shores of the Red Sea, or echoed through the hill country round about Jerusalem.

"Then sang Moses and the children of Israel this song unto the Lord, saying, I will sing unto the Lord, for he hath triumphed gloriously." [4]

That was from the men. And answering them came the softer voices of
Miriam and "all the women," cheering them on:

"Sing ye to the Lord, for he hath triumphed gloriously." [5]

This was no written music they had met to practise; it was fresh out of their hearts; with all their enemies "dead upon the shore," and Israel free.

Or listen to the chorus of women that "came out of all the cities of Israel" to meet the army, when David had conquered the Philistine in single-handed fight.

"And the women answered one another as they played, and said,

"Saul hath slain his thousands"—

"And David his ten thousands"—

You perceive that they understood music in those days; every word in the great swell of song so distinct, that Saul heard every word—and "was very wroth."

So "at the dedication of the wall of Jerusalem" (think of *dedicating* a city wall! how they must have believed Ps. 127) the dedication was kept

"With gladness, both with thanksgiving, and with singing, with cymbals, psalteries, and harps." [6]

And as the bands of people went up to Jerusalem to the three great feasts, they sang and chanted from time to time as they marched along, the Levites at their head beginning the song, and the rest joining in.

"I was glad when they said unto me—" [7]

"As the mountains are round about Jerusalem" [8]—and all the rest. Ah what music! You see the Bible is a great favourer of sweet sounds.

But all this, you will say, was public and special,—not meant for recreation. Let us listen to the Bible music which is private and personal, and you will find it every bit as sweet.

"Praise the Lord with harps. Sing unto him with the psaltery and an instrument of ten strings. Sing unto him a new song; play skilfully with a loud noise." [9]

Are you not glad of that word "skilfully"? You see you may cultivate your talent to the last point, and may have any amount of new music. The Lord's people are not meant to be bunglers, in any line. And yet some seem to think it is no matter how they sing holy words! This "new song" may perhaps be what David speaks of in another place:

"He hath put a new song in my mouth, even praise unto our God." [10]

For as "his mercies are new every morning," [11] so should also our praises be; new, fresh, vigorous; not always the same old words to the same old tune. "The songs of Zion," so sung, are wondrously sweet; even the poor captives in Babylon were called upon to sing them for the pleasure of their heathen captors.

"The songs of Zion." Many of you imagine they are all pretty much alike; all solemn and tedious and slow. But listen.

"I will sing unto the Lord, because he hath dealt bountifully with me." [12]

Can anything be gayer than that? Or anything sweeter than this:

"My heart is fixed, O God, my heart is fixed: I will sing and give praise." [13]

Or where will you find richer chords that this:

"I will sing of thy power, yea, I will sing of thy mercy in the morning: for thou hast been my defence and refuge in the day of my trouble." [14]

New, skilful, and then comes in another requirement; songs should be sensible.

"I will sing with the spirit, and I will sing with the understanding also." [15]

Know what you sing. Does this keep out all *but* sacred music? I should not think that. But it *does* forbid singing you know not what in a foreign tongue, or mere dead nonsense in your own. I cannot see, for my part, why it is much better to sing "idle words" than to say them. How vapid, how senseless, is many a song one hears from a pretty mouth and a sweet voice. And in music as elsewhere, there is no middle ground: whatever does not edify—build up—pulls down.

"It is better to hear the rebuke of the wise, than for a man to hear the song of fools." [16]

How run the directions?

"Singing and making melody in your hearts to the Lord." [17]

Can you do that? If not, music is no true recreation to you. Whatever chills your feeling for eternal things, making them seem dull and far away, is no breath of life-refreshment, but comes bearing the fumes of death.

Do you think you would never sing at all, unless you sometimes forgot such solemn thoughts? Ah there you are mistaken.

"Behold, my servants shall sing for joy of heart." [18]

Not forgetfully, but in full remembrance.

"Is any merry? let him sing psalms." [19]

"Thy statutes have been my songs in the house of my pilgrimage." [20]

Now somebody will say that I have wandered quite away from recreation, and gone off to church. But no; I am speaking of heart and home music. You all know that there is no *recreation* about most of your music now-a-days. You bore yourselves and other people with much practising, and when you have learned, as you think, then you drop it all. Who is ready with a song for some weary, tuneless life? or who "keeps up her music" till the tired years of her own? Work for it, pay for it, drop it, — that is the record. Your music, as it is, is a dead thing; and I want you to put the principle of life in it. For whatever you begin for your Master, you will also hold fast for him.

Read over these words and ponder them well:

"He that had received the five talents, went and traded with the same, and made them other five talents." [21]

Every gift the man had, was used for Christ.

How precious a gift this musical power is! how usable a gift.

"A very lovely song of one that hath a pleasant voice, and can play well on an instrument." [22]

How much it can do for ourselves, for the world.

"David took an harp, and played with his hand; so Saul was refreshed, and was well, and the evil spirit departed from him." [23]

I have never forgotten how a lady with no great musical skill or education sang a verse of a hymn for me one night. It was at a little party, so she could not raise her voice above the softest undertone; but she sang that verse just to let me hear the tune, which I did not know. The words were familiar:

"There is a fountain filled with blood" —

I suppose I have often heard them what you call "better sung"; but never with more lovely effect. Every word, every note, was absolutely distinct and clear, yet not one rising above that undertone: I doubt if even the people nearest to us heard; and the most restless nerves, the weariest head, could have listened and been refreshed. I know my eyes grew full; and I thought to myself, "Ah, you have practised your voice by many a sick bed, and trained it for just that work."

"The evil spirit departed from Saul." But what of music that puts the evil spirit into men? Of songs, however sweet sounding, that are written in the service of the devil, and sung at the high court of the world? For this is your rule:

"Singing with grace in your hearts to the Lord." [24]

Like your speech, "alway with grace."

[1] I Chron. xiii. 8.

[2] Ps. lxviii. 25, 26.

[3] I Chron. xv. 16.

[4] Ex. xv. 1.

[5] Ex. xv. 21.

[6] Neh. xii. 27.

[7] Ps. cxxii. 1.

[8] Ps. cxxv. 2.

[9] Ps. xxxliii. 2, 3.

[10] Ps. xl. 3.

[11] Lam. iii. 13.

[12] Ps. xiii. 6.

[13] Ps. lvii. 7.

[14] Ps. lix. 16.

[15] I Cor. xiv. 15.

[16] Eccle. vii. 5.

[17] Eph. v. 19.

[18] Isa. lxv. 14.

[19] James v. 13.

[20] Ps. cxix. 54.

[21] Matt. xxv. 16.

[22] Ez. xxxiii. 32.

[23] I Sam. xvi. 23.

[24] Col. iii. 16.

Dancing

"To everything there is a season, and a time to every purpose under heaven." [1]

And so it comes among the rest, that there is "a time to dance." [2] Such being the case, we have only to find out the when and the how; for of course, for Christians, dancing too must have its rules. In feasting the word is, "Do all to the glory of God"; and in music, "With melody in your hearts to the Lord"; and now for dancing the order comes:

"Let them praise his name in the dance." [3]

We are to praise the Lord with our whole lives; in our recreation no less than in our work. You see it is all one: with that proviso you may do anything.

"Praise him for his mighty acts: praise him according to his excellent greatness."

"Praise him with the timbrel and dance." [4]

I fancy you did not expect this, secretly believing that the Bible was all against dancing. I fancy most people would start back and say it cannot be done. *If* it cannot, or if by *you* it cannot, then—for you—the dancing question should be settled once and for all. The Lord has given you "the garment of praise for the spirit of heaviness," [5] and you are not at liberty to lay it off for any dancing gear whatever.

"Ye are a chosen generation, a royal priesthood, an holy nation, a peculiar people; that ye should shew forth the praises of him who hath called you out of darkness into his marvellous light." [6]

The condition is absolute; and all doubts upon the dancing question are at an end for you. But for those who like to inquire into possibilities, let us search a little further. "Praise him in the dance."—Has it ever been done? Never,—in such dances as you are accustomed to. But a great while ago, on the shores of the Red Sea, while the men were chanting the praises of that God who had brought them safe out of Egypt, the women banded together "with timbrels and with dances" [7] (no *mixed* dances, observe), and so, dancing for joy at the great deliverance, answered the men, chorus like:

"Sing ye to the Lord, for he hath triumphed gloriously." [8]

So after Jephthah's victory,[9] came out his daughter to meet him "with timbrels and with dances."

So after the rout of the Philistines,

"The women came out of all the cities of Israel, singing and dancing, to meet king Saul." [10]

And though praise of the human agents mingled in, yet only Divine power had won the day, and well they knew it. And again you remember how when the ark was brought home to Jerusalem,

"David danced before the Lord with all his might." [11]

Does it seem very strange to you? So it did to David's wife on that occasion; for as she had no praise in her heart, no sympathy with the joy, of course the expression of it tried her patience. Dancing for joy,—we often use the image, but these people did the thing. It is hard enough to keep still sometimes, if one is very happy.

Not like our dancing!—you say. Indeed not much. No special steps, no intricate figures, no elaborate positions, no dressing for effect. David even laid his royal robes aside, instead of putting them on; they were in his way. How could one dance for joy in a state dress? No need of partners, where every one danced for glad thankfulness of heart. No "envy, malice, and all uncharitableness" stirred up by another's dancing or another's dress; no "wall-flowers," no monopoly. No late hours, leaving mind and body jaded for the next day's work. I think "dancing before the Lord" must have been very pure refreshment. And by the way, speaking of dress, I feel, somehow, as if—would people but choose their ornaments out of that treasure-chest of jewels "a meek and quiet spirit," ball dresses would lose their charm, and the German its great attraction. One never likes to go where one's dress is out of keeping.

Christian dancing, for Christian joy. There was music and dancing, as well as feasting, when the prodigal son came home; returned from his sins, washed from his defilement, clothed at last in "the best robe" a sinner can wear.[12] According to the word:

"Thou hast turned for me my mourning into dancing." [13]

Is such glad thankfulness so rare in our days that people have forgotten how it acts? And would such dancing be possible now? I do not know. But answer this question, and you settle at once the other perplexity whether Christians may dance. For there is no other sort of dancing permitted to them, than this which springs up out of the mercies of the Lord, and is all consecrated to his praise.

it is not quite the only sort mentioned in the Bible; but the others do not look attractive upon paper. One of them indeed comes more properly under another head, and the rest are all idolatrous; in the service and honour of that biggest idol, the world; whether any special graven image was set up or not. Dances indulged in only by heathen, or by nominal Christians who had swerved from their allegiance.

When Moses tarried long in the mount, receiving his orders, the people, you remember, grew tired and restless,—in want of recreation, we should call it now,—and then they "quickly corrupted themselves." Weary of waiting, impatient of the monotony of their life, out of their own possessions they made themselves an idol, and then—danced before it! conducting themselves as well became those who had chosen a god that could neither hear nor see.

"The people sat down to eat and drink, and rose up to play." [14]

And you will find this is always just what people do after unhallowed recreation: they *never* rise up to do good work. Test your amusements by that. Recreation *should* be a re-creation to every noble end.

Neither joy, nor thankfulness, nor the unbending from labour, was there among those poor Israelites—those people of the Lord in name; but only lawless mirth and unhallowed indulgence.

"He saw the calf and the dancing, and Moses' anger waxed hot." [15]

You think I am very hard upon dancing; and I have reason. "Two years ago," said a young girl to me, "you told me that if I went on doing these things I should myself change; that I *could* not do them, and keep myself. I was almost angry then, but do you know it has come true? I *have* changed. Things that I minded and shrank from then, I never notice now. I have got used to them, as you said. It frightens me when I think of it." Poor child!—neither fright nor warning have stayed her course since then. A ceaseless thirst for excitement, an endless round of unsatisfying pleasure—so called,—a weary, old, disappointed look on the young face; broken engagements, forgotten promises, a wasted life,—this is what it has all come to. "Hard upon dancing"? yes, I certainly have reason. Do I not find it right in the way of some of my Bible Class who might else become Christians? do I not know how it tarnishes the Christian profession of others? Do not the careless young men in the class boast that they can get the Church members to go with them anywhere—for a dance? Or how would you like to have a young girl come to you, frightened at things she had permitted at a ball the night before, entreating to know if you thought them "*very* bad"?

Examine it, test it for yourself; only be honest. Can you dance "in armour"? crowned and shielded and shining with "the hope of salvation," with "righteousness" and "faith"? Are your shoes "peace"? peace of heart, of conscience. Is your belt the girdle of "truth"? Can you "shew your colours" in the throng? *Dare* you? Are they not rather trailing in the dust, or quietly pocketed, or left at home? Think honestly, and answer to yourself how it is. As in feasting, so here: you cannot dance all night with people, and next day warn them against "the world, and the things of the world," and even hope to be listened to. "I am as good as most Church members,"—ah how often we teachers and talkers meet that rebuff! And how well the Lord knew when he said:

"He that is not with me, is against me."

"Doth a fountain send forth at the same place sweet water and bitter?" [16]

"A time to dance."—Yes: whenever, and wherever, you can do it as the whole-souled servant of Christ. And how about dancing at home, among ourselves, as people say?—Without going any further, one thing forbids it all. If you dance anywhere,—you, a professing Christian,—in the eyes of the world you dance *everywhere*.

The world allows no middle ground for Christians. "I saw her danc-ing,"—and nobody stops to inquire when, or with whom, or how. So that there is nothing for you but this:

"Avoid it, pass not by it, turn from it, and pass away." [17]

[1] Eccle. iii. 1.

[2] Eccle. iii. 4.

[3] Ps. cxlix. 3.

[4] Ps. cl. 2, 4.

[5] Isa. lxi. 3.

[6] I Pet. ii. 9.

[7] Ex. xv. 20.

[8] Ex. xv. 20.

[9] Judges xi. 3.

[10] I Sam. xviii. 6

[11] II Sam. vi. 14.

[12] Luke xv. 11.

[13] Ps. xxx. 11.

[14] Ex. xxxii. 6

[15] Ex. xv. 19.

[16] James iii. 11.

[17] Prov. iv. 15.

Theatres.

If I say that it degrades oneself to find pleasure in degrading things or degraded people, you will perhaps admit the fact but deny that it has any application to theatre-going. Is it not a fashionable, intellectual, and what not, amusement? Let us see.

Many of you who yet are theatre-goers, know well that you would feel yourselves degraded if even a dear friend went on the stage.

"She has trailed an honoured name in the dust,"—so have I heard the comment, from one who was not even a personal friend. "She might at least have taken another name!"—And the speaker was not brought up among Puritans, and belonged to a Church which—as a Church—has no fear of the theatre. I think occasional indulgence was common enough in the family. And the young actress had done nothing but become an actress, keeping her own name. Friends are mortified,—and yet friends go to see, and to help along.

"But what shall actors do?" you say; "it is their way of getting a livelihood." No, not if support were given only to *other* ways. A man may make a round sum at a rowing match which cripples his strength for life; or by leaping across Passaic Falls, till he breaks his neck; he may set up for a wizard or a conjuror or a quack doctor,— he may pick your pocket or fire your house,—all in the way of business. The only question is in which way will you help him on. Things must be judged of quite apart from their money-making results. The old African maker of "greegrees" (charms) burns them all when she becomes a Christian; and the young carpenter just converted under Mr. Moody's preaching, gives up his only job because he can not do it for Christ, and will not even drive a nail in the scaffolding about a theatre. For the money that changes hands there, is the price of "the souls of men."

You do not believe all this: you do not believe that evil can hide among such fascinations. And for the actors, they are not men and women! Are they not kings and queens and fairies? The glamour of their dress, the strangeness of the scenes, the un-everyday tragic or fantastic air of it all; with sometimes the witchery of music or the wonders of artistic effect, lay a spell upon your common sense. Do I not know? Have I not seen young Christian girls from the country a standing jest with people who knew the world, because—beginning with what the laughers called "a holy horror" of the theatre—they yielded and went "just once." Then, "only once more,"—and then presently would go every night, to see everything!

When Miriam was six years old, some acquaintances over-persuaded her father to let them take her to see Cinderella,—Cinderella and some part of Der Freischutz; and one who was there remembers well how hard the little hands grasped the edge of the box, and how impossible it was to win the young eyes round, even by a vision of sugarplums. To the end of her life, I fancy, she will see now and then a picture out of that fairyland. Next day Miriam entreated earnestly to have the pleasure over again; strengthening her plea with this remarkable promise, that if she might go once more, she would never do anything wrong again as long as she lived! Her father paced up and down the room with a grave smile upon his lips, the little suppliant following with eager feet, ever renewing her request, and he answering little; for the matter was beyond her ken. But he was a Christian who kept off the Debatable land; and where his foot might not enter, he would not send his child. Had he not himself dedicated her to be the Lord's? She never went again. Never to the theatre; never again to any such place, until long afterwards; and with that going he had nothing to do.

Miriam had grown up, had become a Christian and a happy one; and as yet no "flatterer" had beguiled her off upon the "Enchanted Ground." But at last the temptation came, in a very specious way.

There was a new Prima Donna at the opera house that winter; a young, pretty woman, working hard (it was said) to support her mother; and Miriam, going daily to see dear friends at the same hotel, often heard the singing and practising that went on in the Prima Donna's rooms. And Miriam was very fond of music, and had been able to hear very little that was really good; and now in a moment one thing took possession of her; she *must* go to the opera!—Tickets too costly, and no one to take her, made the thing look impossible on the one side; and on the other—there was her Christian name and promise. Of course it was wrong for Christians to go!—she knew that. Yet for the time, nothing seemed tangible or real but this; go she *must*! And so from week to week this fever of desire grew and increased, fed from time to time by those snatches of song that floated through the great hall of the hotel.

At last one day her friends said (knowing nothing of all this), "Miriam, you must go with us to an undress rehearsal. We have got tickets, and you must go." Then beginning to answer the objections they expected—"It is only undress," they said; "the house half lighted, and the actors not in costume. Anybody might go,—and you *must.*"—"It's a very moral opera," began another. "Of course we would never take you to see anything else."

Miriam was too ignorant of the world and its theatres to fairly understand all these advantages,—indeed I fancy longing made such a din in her ears that she paid but little attention. For a while she withstood—then desire rose up like a whirlwind and carried all before it. They had tickets for that very night,—her friends, said one morning,—a ticket for her also—and an escort. She yielded and went. Went first to take tea with her friends, on the way; and I have heard her speak of the thrilling, pent-up excitement of that hour or two before it was time to set out:—Excitement that made her as still as a mouse, and the careless chatter of her friends incomprehensible!—that made cake into plain bread and butter, and bread and butter into—chips, for all she knew. Whether the excitement was all pleasure I doubt if she could tell; yet if you think Miriam knew she was doing wrong, you would be mistaken. Perhaps it was with her, in the tumult of longing, as Fenelon says: "O how rare it is to find a soul still enough to hear God speak!" Or perhaps the Lord, in his wisdom, chose this time to let her set her own lesson. I can only vouch for the dream in which she sat at tea, and walked along the street, and entered the Opera House; glad to get out into the starlight, almost awe-struck to find herself at last within those walls.

The rehearsal was very "undress" indeed. The house, not half lighted, had yet fewer spectators than jets of gas,—a handful of shadowy figures, hid away by twos and threes in the dim boxes; which were almost too dark for the reading of libretti. However eyes were young, and the party put their heads together and began to study out the coming opera, and so get a taste of the pleasure beforehand. Until—Well, as I said, Miriam was young and ignorant of the World, but a woman's instincts (if they have not been tampered with) outgrow her years and are independent of her experience. And as the girl bent over the libretto, some of these instincts took fright. She found out suddenly that those small pages were not just the reading she liked, with a gentleman looking over her shoulder; and instantly sat back, leaving the rest to their studies, and read not another word that night. She kept still, waiting for the music,— and then the music began.

You who see such places only with all the conjuring power of light and dress upon them, have no idea how they look when things are transformed back again, and Cinderella has lost her glass slippers, and the coach is a pumpkin, and the coachman is a rat. This night the actors came on the stage in more—or less—than ordinary dress; as men look when they have put on their dowdiest, for bad weather or dirty work: and these men wore their hats. Only the young Prima Donna was bare-headed, and of course (being a woman) had not made herself a fright. "Can a maid forget her ornaments?" And this just touched off the effect of all the rest. But the music!—

The many discords and melodies of life since then have at last confused in Miriam's recollection the sounds she listened to that night; but for years liter she could hear them almost as distinctly as at first; and the *picture* has never faded. The slim, fair girl; the rough, unwashed, unkempt-looking men; men whom (had she been *your* sister) you would not have let touch her—as we say—"with a pair of tongs."

The play went on. Perhaps the libretto had given an uneasy stir to Miriam's satisfaction, for as she sat now entranced with the music, suddenly there came to her the astounding revelation that this young girl on the stage, was singing those very words which the other young girl in the boxes had not quite liked to read. Singing them at the top of her sweet voice,—trying to bring them out distinctly and with full effect. It was only a queen, to be sure; but somehow (missing the royal robes) Miriam could see only a woman. Close upon this came another shock. These dingy, untidy, soiled-looking men were now making love to the young Prima Donna,— first one and then another; this one in bass, and that one in baritone, and she answering in her clear soprano. Answering,—sometimes *responding*. Then they touched her, and handled her, and drew her about, as the exigencies of the piece demanded. And there was no glitter of dress to turn the one into a kingly suitor and the other into a faithful knight; the tarnished men were but men; and she—poor little uncrowned princess—was but a woman among them all; rubbing off the bloom and reserve of her woman's nature with every touch.

Miriam could never tell how sick hearted she grew as she looked. *That* was this girl's livelihood; to go through all sorts of situations, with all sorts of men, for the amusement of other people. O yes, it paid well. Had she been a teacher,—had she painted cups or stitched seams for a living,—her salary, her wages, would have been brought down to the lowest figure; but on the stage, at *that* work, give her what she asks!—or make her so popular that the manager will. Does she not "amuse" us all?

If ever anybody was thoroughly cured of theatre going, that was Miriam. It had been the greatest temptation of her life; but now a great recoil came over her, so that from that day, the mere thought of the stage brought only loathing and disgust. And so all women, *as* women, should set their faces against it in every shape; even down to the most "private" of private theatricals. There cannot possibly be a wholesome imitation of a bad thing.

I know it is very unfashionable doctrine. I know that even while I write, the newspapers set forth an advertisement of a play, prepared by a clergyman, to be acted by Sunday Schools in this sweet Christmas time. Alas poor Sunday Schools!—in full training for service under "the world, the flesh, and the devil."—"Feed my lambs," the Lord Jesus said,—and between meals you give them whiskey and water! Nor is it the children only who suffer. I could tell of one lady in that very man's church, who being much delighted with some such performance in the Sunday School, went off the very next night to a theatre, to see the same thing *done better*.

N. B.—She had never been before.

"I will have dances at home for my children, lest they seek them elsewhere."—

"I will take my boys to the theatre, because I do not want them to go anywhere without me."—

Real sayings, of real mothers, church members both. Which sayings, in everyday English, read thus, "Since I want my children to keep out of the world, I will bring the world to them at home."—"Since my boys will do what I do not approve, I will guard them by doing it too." Far different from the strong stern-words of Scripture:

"Come out of her, my people."

"Touch not the unclean thing."

And then the wonderful sayings of Psalm i. 1.

If anybody thinks I have given an unfair instance, or that I characterize it unfairly, let them take other testimony where no prejudice can be supposed. Read Mrs. Kemble's "Journal" of her stage life. Read the opinion she gives of it all in her later "Recollections." Yet from childhood some of her nearest and dearest she had known as actors.

I have spoken first as to people bound by the Golden Rule, and forbidden therefore to help anybody even to get a living in an evil way. For the work the theatre does upon yourselves, you know it, if you will be honest. People answer: "O if it hurt me, of course I would give it up." Be honest with yourself, and you will come out of that delusion. You *know* it does not make love to Christ warmer, or thoughts of heaven sweeter; or the atmosphere of your everyday life more wholesome and sound. You know it leaves a restless craving for excitement,—you know it exalts the world before your eyes; and if you think a little you will find that, like my poor young friend in her dancing, you are not edified, not built up, but pulled down. Let me tell you of one case where the mother was a Church member, and had prayers regularly every morning with her family, But the command to *watch* as well (*i.e.,* "keep awake") she had forgotten. And the desire seized her to see—I will not write the name down here, but it was one of those foreign importations which have beguiled thousands. She did not want her son to know of her going, and so went with her young daughter for escort! But she found her son already there, and for twenty-eight nights running he was there again. Why not?—if his mother went once? And as might be expected, the daughter has become (as people say) "wild for the theatre."

Among the people who loved Mr. Lincoln best, and could best understand the semi-official way in which he went to the theatre that fatal night, there was not one, I fancy, who did not feel an added shock at learning where he was when the messenger came, and who did not wish that he had been almost anywhere else. Yet why? If the theatre is a proper place for Christians to enter, it is as good a place as any other to be

"Waiting — waiting — when the Lord shall come."

The only thing I think of mentioned in the Bible that is much like modern performances on the boards, is the dancing of the daughter of Herodias before Herod. She worked for hire, she beguiled her audience. "She pleased the king," and got from him all she asked for. It sounds very dreadful to you, no doubt, that the prophet's head should have been danced off by a pair of whirling feet? — but that is a slight matter. If dancing and theatre going did only take off the heads of protesting saints, like an old-time persecution, they at least would but exchange the prison for the palace, and so not lose much. But this stealing away the heart and service once vowed to Christ, is another matter. You think it does not do this. You think your eye is as clear for heaven in the boxes as elsewhere. You think you can dress and go and look on and listen, keeping close to this command:

"Whatsoever ye do, in word or deed, do all in the name of the Lord Jesus."

Do you think so?

"I have never been to hear him," said Dr. Skinner, speaking then, only of a false prophet in a false Church, "because I could not expect to meet my Master there; and I will go nowhere for pleasure where he is not." What about the theatre, tried by that test?

How surely the world marks every Christian who is seen at such places; how certainly the children know that the parents have not yet forsaken all for Christ. And how constantly ungodly men fence off your warning, with the words: "Look at — — and — —, I am as good as they. I do this and that, and they do it too. I don't see the difference."

But "nobody knows." O yes, everybody knows. No matter if you are across the sea, — "A bird of the air shall carry the matter." But especially, the Lord knows. He setteth "a print on the heels of my feet" [1] — and step you never so lightly, the mark will be there, and the Lord will know.

And where your feet go, there others will follow. "Is Miss Hope going to such and such a performance?" inquired a young man of me. I said no. He stood gravely thinking, and the talk drifted on. Then suddenly I heard him say — to himself as it were: — "Then I will not go either!" —

Persuasions, entreaties, ridicule, are nothing, *mean* nothing, if only you stand firm. And I have known gentlemen spend their strength in entreaties, and then when the lady held out in her quiet refusal, they said afterwards to other people that they liked to see any one true to his principles.

Staying once with some friends of rather free opinions and practice, Priscilla was beset to go with them on a certain evening to the theatre. So eager were the words, so well-loved the friends, that at last she grew desperate. Turning round upon the head of the house, she said: "Do you really want me to go?" — He looked at her, sat back in his chair in silence, then answered soberly: "Well, I guess I'd just as lieve you didn't!"

Depend upon it, the very people who press you hardest, professing to see "no harm," will feel they have lost something if you make them think the King's Country is just like their own. Whatever has happened to *your* moral sense, *they* know that the theatre is no place for a true-hearted servant of the Lord Jesus, if the Master is all he is represented to be. If they met you there unawares, it would be with a thrill not of pleasure but of pain.

Let me repeat my question, Is it as a Christian you go to the theatre? can you go and keep your armour bright? does the helmet of salvation rest securely on your head? Is the girdle of truth, — truth of life, purpose, and heart, — fast bound? the breastplate of righteousness burnished, the shield of faith ready against every dart that may fly in that great building? Are they the shoes of peace on which you go in? not pleasure, but *peace*? Is it the sword of the Spirit with which you meet and parry the thrusts of idleness, folly, mischief? Ah you know better! When you go to the theatre these defences are left at home, as not fit for the occasion. The house is built and managed and filled in the interests of the enemy; and of course your uniform is out of place. Tired Church members, do you go there for *rest*?

[1] Job xiii. 27.

Games.

Dr. Skinner[1] used to say that all games of chance were unlawful. For inasmuch as there is no chance in the economy of this world, all use of dice or lottery in any shape is really an appeal to him of whom it is said:

"The lot is cast into the lap, but the whole disposing thereof is of the Lord." [2]

And you will agree with me that this is not a thing to be done lightly.

In old times the casting of a lot was a solemn religious service: ushered in even among pagans with prayer and often with fasting; but what careless, reckless ignoring of God as the Governor among the nations, is there in all connected with the lot in our days. What foul associations cloud and wrap up almost every game of chance: how soiled are the cards, how unhallowed the rattle of the dice. What degrading, debasing work is done by every species of lottery; what desperate evils spring up and grow out of "a chance" at a Church fair! Some years ago, at the time of the great German and French fairs in New York, a lady thoughtlessly gave her young son leave to buy "a chance" for a gold watch. Thoughtlessly,—it was just a dollar to the fair and an amusement to the boy. And before twenty-four hours had passed, she would have given anything in the world to recall her permission. For at once the boy's mind became wholly absorbed in his "chance." The fair went on, the drawing was long delayed; and day after day—hour by hour, if he could—he went to inquire and to watch; and the mother saw her child in a true gambling fever, and she obliged to let it run its course. Mercifully, as she said, the watch fell to another. "If it had come to George, I don't know what in the world I should have done."

"We play for sugarplums,"—we "toss up" for nuts; but each time the evil seeds are planted. The mere habit of *talking* of "chance," of "luck," of "fate," as if you believed in them all, tends directly to weaken your realizing trust in the Great Ruler of the world; who counts his sparrows, and numbers the hairs of your head. Chance? If the watchmaker could not control one smallest wheel or point in his watch; if even a grain of dust got in and defied him; what think you he could do with mainspring and hands? One unmanageable atom would stop the whole.

To quote Dr. Skinner again,—one to whom I think it never occurred to like anything but what God liked,—in his early life as a young man he had seen much wild company; and so strong was their association with evil, that to the end of his life he could never even hear the dice fall without a shiver.

"Put it away, my dear," he would say of even the backgammon board. "I don't like it—I don't like it!"

For games of chance, as a rule, gather round them a setting of sin and sorrow which other games do not. I suppose men take in their practical infidelity, and grow lawless. You do not mean to appeal to God in your games of "chance,"—but if not to him, then to some other power supposed to be outside his rule or beyond his notice: "chance," "luck," or the devil. And it does not much matter which word you use. Yet "tired" Church members will play euchre and whist, and there are cards in the table drawer in the parlour, and of course a dingier pack in the kitchen, in many a so-called Christian house; though the family hide them or apologize before people who are called "intense." The minister comes in upon a card party in his parish, and all rise in deprecatory confusion; and perhaps (ah I know it happened in one case) the minister waves his hand graciously, with a "Don't let me disturb you,"—and so passes on. O it hurts one to have a fellow Christian ask in the quiet evening at her own house, "Would you object to our bringing out the cards?"—"I could not touch them," was all the answer, and the drawer stayed shut. But I wish a Nonconformist Church could rise up in these days. We are so busy calling ourselves Episcopalians, Methodists, Presbyterians, that we seem to forget the old far-better name which should include all. In the war it was only loyal or disloyal: and New York was proud of the Wisconsin boys that were all six feet two; and Ohio wept for those of Massachusetts who were among the first to shed their blood. Dear friends, it is war time now: if you could only realize that, a good many things would be set straight. Not able to give up doubtful games and questionable dances? Why in '76 the women fired at their tea kettles!—

Nonconformists. But now, "My mother does it,"—"my aunt goes,"—"my father likes it": so run the excuses which the members of your Bible Class, children of Church members, fling in your face.

But what you call "lawful" games, are stupid. Not all of them, perhaps; but if they were, that would not touch the question. Paul's "If meat make my brother to offend, I will eat no flesh while the world standeth," was crippled with no such condition as "If I can get bread." And when the Lord bade us cut off the offending right hand, no question of whether we could live without it came in. It is not absolutely needful that Christ should find all his tired Church members rested and fresh; but it *is* necessary that they should be "spotless," "faithful," "ready," when he comes.

There are other amusements that might be touched upon just here, but perhaps they are as well not named. Whatever takes you full into the ranks of Christ's enemies, not to fight but to follow them; whatever you cannot do straight through in the name of the Lord Jesus; whatever turns you away from the shining presence of his face; is unlawful for you. Once remember that there is no middle ground, and then ask yourself what standing room there can be for you on a race course, what seat at a circus. If you are not with Christ, openly, unmistakably, you are "scattering," even in your games. I asked a friend (a minister of deep experience) lately, if he had seen much of this private card playing among Church members? He answered, "Yes, a great deal." Then I inquired what was the effect, as he had noticed it. And the reply was instant and emphatic:

"*Always* evil!" —

Carlyle tells of "patriots" in the French Revolution who shaved each other out of the fragments of bomb shells, and wore ghastly trophies from the guillotine. But short of a Reign of Terror, making all men mad, one does not expect such things. Few people (I fancy) if they knew it, would care to use the glass from which some poor wretch had drunk his draught of poison; and even to touch the murderer's knife stored up in a public museum, would turn most hearts sick. But if you could only see as God sees; if things in society were but labelled and classed; you would find your cards dark with the soul-life blood of thousands, and could hear their ruin in every fall of the dice.

I was much interested in a recent English essay ("On the Criminal Code of the Jews") to find how the typical Israel regarded games of chance. As if something of the old blessed "The Lord is our King," staid by them, even in the days of their downfall. The writer says:

"All who made money by dice-playing or any games of hazard, by betting on pigeon matches and similar objectionable practices, were not only incapable of becoming members of a tribunal, but were not permitted to give evidence. The Ghemara regards a man who gains money by the amusements named, as dishonest."

[1] Once pastor of the Mercer Street Church, New York, and Professor in Union Theological Seminary.

[2] Prov. xvi. 33.

What Left?

But you will say, I leave nothing for you, then; no amusements, no recreation. Is that true? Is the narrow way indeed so barren, that we must step out of it to rest? Has the Lord only food and water for his flock, and when they need change and refreshment must they leave their Shepherd, and go over to the wolf for a run upon the hillside? That sounds hard for weak human nature — and strange, for a Lord of boundless resources. And somehow the Bible pictures of the flock shew wondrous contentment. "A stranger will they not follow." [1]

Then following the Master must be very sweet; for all men like variety, and the mere fact of a new voice is of itself enough to draw one aside. Yet "a stranger will they not follow, but will flee from him," — O how much that tells! And here we touch the very root and spring of true refreshment, of real recreation. For while good general health is the best specific against mere bodily fatigue, so against a jaded, over-wrought state of nerves and energies, there is nothing like a heart full of joy and a mind at rest.

"He that believeth on me shall never thirst." [2]

And if this satisfaction does not underlie all your pastimes, they will be a failure. No other stream alone can freshen even the small dry barrens of this earth.

But besides that, what is there left for Christian people?

To begin: "Dancing is such good exercise!" people say. Granted. Or at least it *might* be. But instead of night hours in a ball room, get on horseback for two hours in the open day, and then balance the profit and loss. You don't know how? — then learn. You have no horse? Go to riding school. An hour in the ring will stir your blood better than twenty Germans. But you "cannot afford" to take riding lessons. — Well to say nothing of ball dresses, just throw satin slippers and long gloves and carriage hire together, and see if you cannot afford it. Ay, and have a ticket now and then for some one poorer than yourself.

Then for people who live within reach of the opera, there is generally much other good music to be had, at far less expense and with none of the objections. And there again, the money and time spent at the opera, would train the voices at home into a lovely choir. Voices which now "have no time," and talents perhaps un-known.

"Everybody cannot sing."—No. And neither can everybody paint; but it is a delicious pleasure to those who can. What joy to go sketching! what delight to work up the sketches at home. What pure, noiseless, exquisite play it is. And if some of the party care nothing for pencils, let them lie under a tree with a book, and be part of your picture.

"Ah, books!—Of course you disapprove of novels,"—some one exclaims.

Indeed no. A good novel is very improving as well as refreshing. And after much study over that word "good" (that is, for us, worth reading) I can give no better meaning than this. A good book, whether novel or other, is one which leaves you further on than it took you up. If when you drop it, it drops you, right down in the same old spot; with no finer outlook, no cleared vision, no stimulat-ed desires, it is in no sense a good book for you. As well make fancy loaves of sawdust, and label them "Good Bread"; and claim that you rise from the banquet refreshed.

A novel has special power of its own. It may be deeply historical, like "Waverly," and "The Tale of Two Cities." It may be a picture of vivid local colouring, like "Ivanhoe," or "Lorna Doone," or "Dr Antonio." It may be full of social hints and glimpses, with many a cov-ert wise suggestion, like Miss Austin's "Emma." It may shew up a vital truth or a life-long mistake, like Miss Edgeworth's "Helen," or open out new natural scenes like the "Adventures of a Phaeton"; or life scenes, like "Oliver Twist"; or be so full of frolic and fun and sharp common sense, that the mere laughter of it does you good "like a medicine." Witness "Christie Johnstone," and Miss Carlen's "John." All such books are utterly helpful, and leave you well in advance of where they found you. They enlarge your world, they stimulate your life. Only read none that enlarge it by a peep through the gates of hell. On *that* side knowledge is death.

But how is one to tell? you ask. Books are not labelled "good," "bad," and "indifferent." No: and when you go to shops and houses you do not know what air you will find, perhaps not till you open the door. But you start back from one room, and hold your breath in another, hastening to get away; not because you have studied chemistry and can analyze the air, but because your keen physical sense is smitten. Keep your moral sense as fresh, as keen; and the moment you find foul air in a book, throw the book in the fire. Do not leave it about to poison some one else. And if you find no wholesome stir, no real refreshment, but only a feverish thirst beginning, lay the book down: remember, you are after *recreation*.

Re-creation,—the remaking and refitting of ourselves for better work, the resting for more labour, the learning, that we may grow thereby. *That* is what you profess to need, dear fellow Christians. Then seek it,—and take no makebelieve.

"Nothing left?"—Why the world is so full of delightful things to do, that one can but look at a quarter of them. They stand at my elbow ten deep. Books and music, and painting, and riding, and gardening, with all sorts of studies of the wonderful works of God. You are not shut up to novels. Books of art, books of travel, books of poetry, books of science. O how I have rested in the coolness of Longfellow's "Cathedral"; and with what delight seen Alpine heights with Ruskin.

Then there is that wonder of refreshment, the stereoscope. One comes back from a half hour there in a Swiss valley as into a new world, with the dust all blown away. A stereoscope costs little, and views are not expensive,—that is if you are content with one or two at a time, which is the real way to buy them; choosing, considering, carefully selecting only those you cannot possibly go home without! I know we began with six; those six sorted out with jealous care from the contents of many boxes; and by ones and twos the little collection has grown into something worth having. And if you turn over every lot of views you come across, you will often find one rare and fine and cheap, thrown in among the rubbish.

Then there is the microscope,—full of rich pleasure and deep study and wonderful revealings. And here again no great outlay is needed. The days of only sixty dollar glasses are quite gone by, and for five or ten dollars—even less—you can get a microscope that will keep ahead of you for some time to come.

On the other hand, if one has neither the skill nor the means to furnish a home-made telescope, there are other ways of studying the stars, from the days of Ferguson down. You remember he used to measure the distance from star to star with beads upon a string. I have seen a man who could neither read nor write, and yet could tell by the stars the hour at any time of night; and it is a shame that we educated people who know so much, should also know so little.

If you are in the country, and fond of "stones," get a geologist's hammer, and Hugh Miller's books, and give yourself up to happiness. Or if you like flowers, study *them*; learning to know families and sub-families through all the floral peerage.

But perhaps you "do not care for out-door things?" Then get a bit of wood and a few carving tools, and see what dainty wonders you can make at home. Or lose your cares in "illuminating"; or bury them fathom deep in German. From any of these, well begun and carried on, you will come back re-created for your work: made over "as good as new." Not poisoned with bad air, nor wearied by late hours; not singed and jaded with chagrin, vanity, and disappointment. Riding, rowing, archery, fishing, ought to give Christian people enough exercise, without their being obliged to frequent ball rooms to find it; and as for the "grace" people talk of, nothing teaches that like a heart full of graces — "love, joy, peace," and the rest. Do *they* flourish at your doubtful entertainments? do they not rather droop and hang their heads, like the dear flowers in your bouquet?

And if people sought their refreshment among all those sweet and wholesome things, conversation would no longer be the difficult and the dry thing it is in many a company. There would be something to talk about worth talking of; and men of sense would venture to talk sense, even to women; and gossip would go down. How much more interesting is a butterfly, than the curtains of the house across the way! —

The world is full of joys and pleasures and wonders, even yet, outside of Eden. So full that as I said, you can only begin to taste them all, in all your life. I think it is stated that no ordinary life-term would suffice for the thorough study of merely the great family of orchids. And all these things which I have named (the list is really much longer), yes, every one of them, rightly used, will ennoble you, and build you up, and refresh you, with every time of using. Not like the snail which crawled up three feet every day and fell back two feet every night: onward and upward shall be your course; with soul and body and mind re-created, restored by right means, to right ends. Only make one rule to yourself: where anything is doubtful, let it alone.

If you tell me I do not know the fascination of these other things, I tell you that I do; and in one line at least have known it as deeply as any one could. But I have also known, that with the coming of Christ into my heart, with the new knowledge of his presence, the old taste fell dead in a moment, and never arose again. I cannot say it was not much to give up, for it was *nothing*. The former fascination fell off, like the dry skin of a chrysalis when the butterfly spreads its wings. And here we reach the very point of the whole difficulty. For with all their crosses, privations, and givings-up, the Lord's people are not meant to dwell in any land of darkness or of drought. Listen to some of the promises.

"The righteous shall hold on his way, and he that hath clean hands shall be stronger and stronger." [3]

"They go from strength to strength." [4]

"They that wait on the Lord shall renew their strength." [5]

For why?

"For the joy of the Lord is your strength." [6]

I believe the words are true for the body as for the mind. It is nowhere promised that you shall not be tired; but so waiting, so living, so abiding by the head waters of all strength, the most lovely, fresh, ever-renewed life shall be yours.

"The righteous shall flourish like the palm tree." [7]

"Their souls shall be as a watered garden." [8]

It is the man "whose delight is in the law of the Lord" who not only "bringeth forth his fruit in his season," but also when the time for freshness and life and growth seems over,

"They shall still bring forth fruit in old age." [9]

Not only "created in Christ Jesus unto good works," but perpetually recreated in him, from hour to hour, from year to year. Has he not said: "I will be as the dew unto Israel"? [10] No more age for them, thus dwelling in "the power of an endless life";[11] no empty hands, for those who "have all things, and abound." [12] No disgust of life or hopelessness of labour for servants who every now and then—from the midst of their work—follow the Master (but only him) "apart to rest awhile," [13] "A stranger will they not follow." You have seen such people; you may see them every now and then; with smooth brows and sweet faces and eyes full of the peace of God.

"And I said, This is the rest, and this is the refreshing." [14]

I am persuaded, that without this, all forms of recreation that can be tried will be but as quack medicines, giving a temporary relief, only to be followed by a sorer need. And while there are a hundred lawful, sweet, wholesome means of rest at our disposal, I believe that even they will fail if used alone. And if you throw in all unlawful pleasures also, the failure will but be the more complete, "All my springs are in thee," [15] and these other things are but channels through which may flow the loving kindness of the Lord. From him comes all your skill to study, your power to sing: the ingenious fancy, the quick intellect, the deft hand, are all his gift. In this exquisite world of his wherein you work, his power, his care, his laws are around you as surely when you play as when you work. So that you can walk with Christ always, as you are meant to do; looking up to him from relaxation as from labour, thus missing the intoxication of the one and forgetting the toil of the other.

Now whatever lawful things such a disciple may "amuse" himself with, you can see at once that for even the doubtful he could have no relish; counting them but as a draught from that "troubled sea whose waters cast up mire and dirt." [16] Neither would he come to his recreations tired of life, nor because his daily round had turned to "white of egg";[17] but with genuine, honest fatigue, taking amusement as he takes sleep, and going back from it with a joyous rebound to his special weedy corner in the vineyard.

"I know I am getting rested," I heard a minister once say in his vacation, "for I am getting hungry for my work!"

"My people have forgotten their resting place"—let it not ever be said of you and me.

But it is those not merely "planted in the courts of the Lord," but who "flourish" there, that are the trees whose "leaf shall not wither"; and in this you have the whole story. A Christian who is *flourishing* where he belongs, will never go where he does *not* belong. And no one who is dwelling daily in the clear sunshine of Christ's presence, will need a dance to enliven him, or a horse race—or a walking match—to keep up his interest in life. There will be "melody in his heart" without the opera; and life will be full and bright and strong, without a speck of tinsel pleasure. Work will be sweet, and play will be joyous; and by one and by the other the man will *grow*—

"Grow, like the cedar in Lebanon."

Now that you may prove all this, that you may begin right, be careful to take the full good of all the ordered resting times: to wit, the Sundays. I wish all tired people did but know the infinite rest there is in fencing off the six days from the seventh. In anchoring the business ships of your daily life as the Saturday draws to its close, leaving them to ride peacefully upon the flow or the ebb until Monday morning comes again. O the delight, the lull, of feeling: "No need to settle this question—no need to think of this piece of work—for a whole long, sweet thirty-six hours!" Why do you take Sunday papers, to keep your nerves astir with business on the Lord's own day of rest? Why do you add up and consult and consider in the pauses of the sermon, or make opportunity for a business whisper in the porch, and on the way home? Why do you let the perplexities of servants, of means, of plans, ruffle your spirits on the one great day of freedom? Do not you know that even a debtor may walk abroad on Sunday, with no fear of a prison; and house doors may stand open, and no sheriff can enter. Shall it be worse with your mind than with your body?

"Sleep, sleep to-day, tormenting cares,
Of earth and folly born,"—

It is the high court of the Prince of Peace.

"Rest on Sunday!"—I hear some earnest worker cry. "Why Sunday is the hardest of all the week!"

Yes, in a way that is true, for workers in the Lord's work. Yet as far as possible do not make it so. Do not imagine that you have the whole world on your shoulders: do not try to have. Do not lift up a burden you can by no means bear. The messengers came back to the Lord with their reports, — so you.

"Lord, they will not hear — "

"Lord, it is done." —

Work with your whole heart and strength; but then take work and class, and lay them at the Lord's feet; and with them the tired worker too. So doing your work peacefully. And if Monday morning finds you tired, it will find you also rested. The air of the world will have cleared somewhat, giving a nearer view of "the city"; its mountains will have sunk down well nigh out of sight, before the everlasting hills to which you may lift up your eyes for help. And labour and care and profit and loss will cease to be a tangle when stamped with this order:

"Occupy till I come."

But for you who are *not* workers (the why and wherefore are for yourselves to say) do you too make the Sabbath a day of rest. Yet do not let your Sunday rest run into Sunday dissipation by trying to hear all the good sermons at once. Choose (and abide by) some true church so near that no street car shall be run for you, and yet — if possible — far enough off to give you a freshening walk as you go and come. Neither take out your carriage, "that thine ox and thine ass may rest." [18] Of course I speak only of places where it is possible to walk to church.

Get up early enough to have no hurry and no "late." Have a simple church dress that will need no fussing; have a simple breakfast, without "hot cakes," and a cold dinner, "that thy man servant and thy maid servant may rest as well as thou." [19]

I know it is charged upon the men of the family that they will never "stand" a cold dinner. But I have catered for just such many times, and I know they will. Only be you careful on Saturday, to provide a dainty repast that is *fit* to eat cold — and then see. You will find those very grumblers charmed with their dinner, and praising it before any other in the week. You can always grace your cold dishes with hot coffee and baked potatoes.

O the rest, the "recreation" of such a day! With all earth's turmoil pushed aside, and Christ himself the one invited guest. Unless indeed some needy friend, who can have no "Sunday" elsewhere. People talk in these days with horror of the old Puritan sabbath. But even if everything be true that they tell of it, I would rather spend Sunday with blinds shut and pictures turned to the wall, than in the full week-day glare which fills some houses. And if you want refreshment from your play-times in the week, if you want heart and mind and face to keep fresh, begin the week with the Lord's day kept wholly to the Lord.

"Verily, my sabbaths ye shall keep: for it is a sign between me and you throughout your generations." [20]

A sabbath, a rest. Rest of mind which lingering in bed will not give; rest of body which feasting could only hinder; a rest of heart by dwelling all day in the deep shadow of the Lord's presence. So beginning the week, this promise shall be upon you as each day rolls on,

"My presence shall go with thee, and I will give thee rest." [21]

"And in all things that I have said unto you be circumspect; and make no mention of the name of other gods, neither let it be heard out of thy mouth." [22]

[1] John x. 5.

[2] John vi. 35.

[3] Job xvii. 9.

[4] Ps. lxxxiv. 7.

[5] Isa. xl. 31.

[6] Neh. viii. 10.

[7] Ps. xcii. 12.

[8] Jer. xxxi. 12.

[9] Ps. xcii. 14.

[10] Hosea xiv. 5.

[11] Heb. vii. 16.

[12] Phil. iv. 18.

[13] Mark vi. 31.

[14] Isa. xxviii. 12.

[15] Ps. lxxxvii. 7.

[16] Isa. lvii. 20.

[17] Job vi. 6.

[18] Ex. xxii 12.

[19] Deut. v. 14.

[20] Ex. xxxi. 13.

[21] Ex. xiii. 14.

[22] Ex. xxiii. 13.